P9-DNB-589

TURTLE DREAMS

TURTLE DREAMS

by Marion Dane Bauer

illustrated by
Diane Dawson Hearn

Holiday House/New York

For Bryan,
Dream on! M. D. B.

With thanks to Liza, D. D. H.

Printed in the United States of America
FIRST EDITION

Library of Congress Cataloging-in-Publication Data
Bauer, Marion Dane.
Turtle dreams / by Marion Dane Bauer: illustrated by Diane Dawson Hearn.
p. cm.
Summary: Turtle talks to different animals about the coming winter, trying to find a dream that will fit her and prepare her for the long cold season of darkness.
ISBN 0-8234-1322-5 (reinforced)
[1. Turtles—Fiction. 2. Animals—Fiction. 3. Winter—Fiction. 4. Dreams—Fiction.] I. Hearn, Diane Dawson, ill. II. Title.
PZ7.B3262Tu 1997 97-2213 CIP AC
[E]—dc21

CONTENTS

1. Winter is Coming

A young turtle lay on a warm rock
at the edge of a cool pond.
She stretched her neck.
She twitched her tail.

She wiggled inside her shell.

"It is fine being a turtle," she said, closing her eyes.

"Winter is coming," a cracked voice cried.

"Are you prepared?"

Turtle's eyes flew open.
Great-great-great Grandmother swam past.

"What is winter?" Turtle asked.

"Winter is cold," Great-great-great Grandmother answered.

"Winter is darkness.

"Winter is the time of the long, long sleep."

Cold?

Darkness?

The long, long sleep?

Turtle shivered.

She called after her great-great-
great grandmother.
"Tell me. How can I prepare?"

“Go gather dreams,” Great-great-great Grandmother called back.
Then she dived beneath the water,
sank to the bottom of the pond,
and buried herself in the mud.

“Dreams!” Turtle cried.
“What are they?
“Where can I find a good one?
“What will I do with it once it is mine?”
A bubble rose to the top of the pond.
But it gave no answer.

"Never mind," Turtle said.
"There must be a dream out there
just right for a young turtle.
"I will go looking.
"When I find it, I will carry it
back on my shell."

So she plopped off the rock.
She swam to the shore.
She climbed the muddy bank.
Winter was coming!
She must prepare.

2. Otter

Otter poked his head out of a hole in the bank.

"Tell me, Otter," Turtle said.

"What is winter?"

Otter winked.

"Winter is snow," he said.

"Winter is ice.

"Winter is fun."

"Do you have a dream for winter?"

Turtle asked.

Otter smiled.

Then he chuckled.

Then he laughed.

"I dream of playing," he said.

"What else?"

"Playing what?" Turtle asked.

"I slide down a frozen bank.

"I skid on the ice.

"I turn flips in the snow,"

Otter told her.

Turtle sighed.

"Your dream will not do for me,"
she said.
"Turtles seldom slide.
"We do not even skid.
"And if we roll over,
getting up is hard."

So she plodded off through
the long grass.
Winter was coming.
She had to find a dream to carry
back on her shell.

3. Squirrel

A few steps from the pond,
Turtle met a squirrel.
"Please," Turtle begged.
"Tell me about winter."
"No, no, no!" Squirrel scolded.

"Do not, not, not ask me
about winter.
"Winter is bare trees.
"Winter is wind.
"Winter is hunger.
"I am much too busy to talk
about winter."

"Can you tell me about dreams then?"
Turtle asked.

"No, no, no!" Squirrel scolded again.

"Dreams are for stormy days.

"Dreams are for freezing nights.

"Dreams are for folks far less busy
than I."

"But what do you dream on
stormy days?" Turtle asked.

"What do you dream on freezing
nights?

"I must know."

"I dream, dream, dream of climbing,"
Squirrel replied.
"I climb to the farthest tip of the
highest branch of the tallest tree
in the entire forest."
Turtle sighed once more.
No turtle she knew could
climb a tree.
"So what do you do there?"
she asked.
"Nuts!" Squirrel said.
"What?" Turtle asked.
"Nuts! Nuts! Nuts!" Squirrel
repeated. "I nibble nuts."

“Oh,” said Turtle.

And she sighed yet again.

This was no dream to carry home

on her shell for winter.

How could she nibble nuts?

Turtles have no teeth.

No teeth at all.

Turtle plodded on.

4. Bird

One step.
Two steps.
Three steps. Four.
Turtle met a bird.

“I need a dream for winter,”
Turtle said.
“Do you have one I could carry
home on my shell?”
“Winter?” Bird clicked his bright
beak.
“Winter is long.
“Winter is cruel.
“Winter is—”
“I know,” Turtle interrupted.
“Winter is cold and dark.
“Winter is ice and snow.
“Winter is bare trees and wind
and hunger.”

"Right!"

Bird blinked a bright eye.

"You know all about winter."

"But my great-great-great grand-mother sent me to gather winter dreams," Turtle said. "And I cannot find one that fits a turtle."

Bird smoothed his bright feathers.
"Birds have the best dreams of all,"
he said.
"Please, tell me yours," Turtle begged.

"I like to dream about
leaving home," Bird said.
"Leaving home!" Turtle cried.
"Yes," Bird replied.
"I stand on the edge of the nest.
"I spread my wings.
"I drop.
"And the good air lifts me.
"Flying is always fine," he said.
"But the first time . . . ah, the very
first time . . . I live it again
and again in my dreams."

Turtle said nothing at all.
She just turned and dragged her
heavy shell back toward the pond.
Turtles cannot fly.
They cannot even leave home.
Not ever.
Their homes go with them
wherever they go.

5. The Best Dream of All

The young turtle sank
to the bottom of the pond.
She buried herself in the mud.
"Great-great-great Grandmother
was wrong," she said.
"There are no winter dreams
for turtles."

She pulled her head and her legs
and her tail inside her shell.
Then she closed her eyes.
She went to sleep.

Where she dreamed of waking.

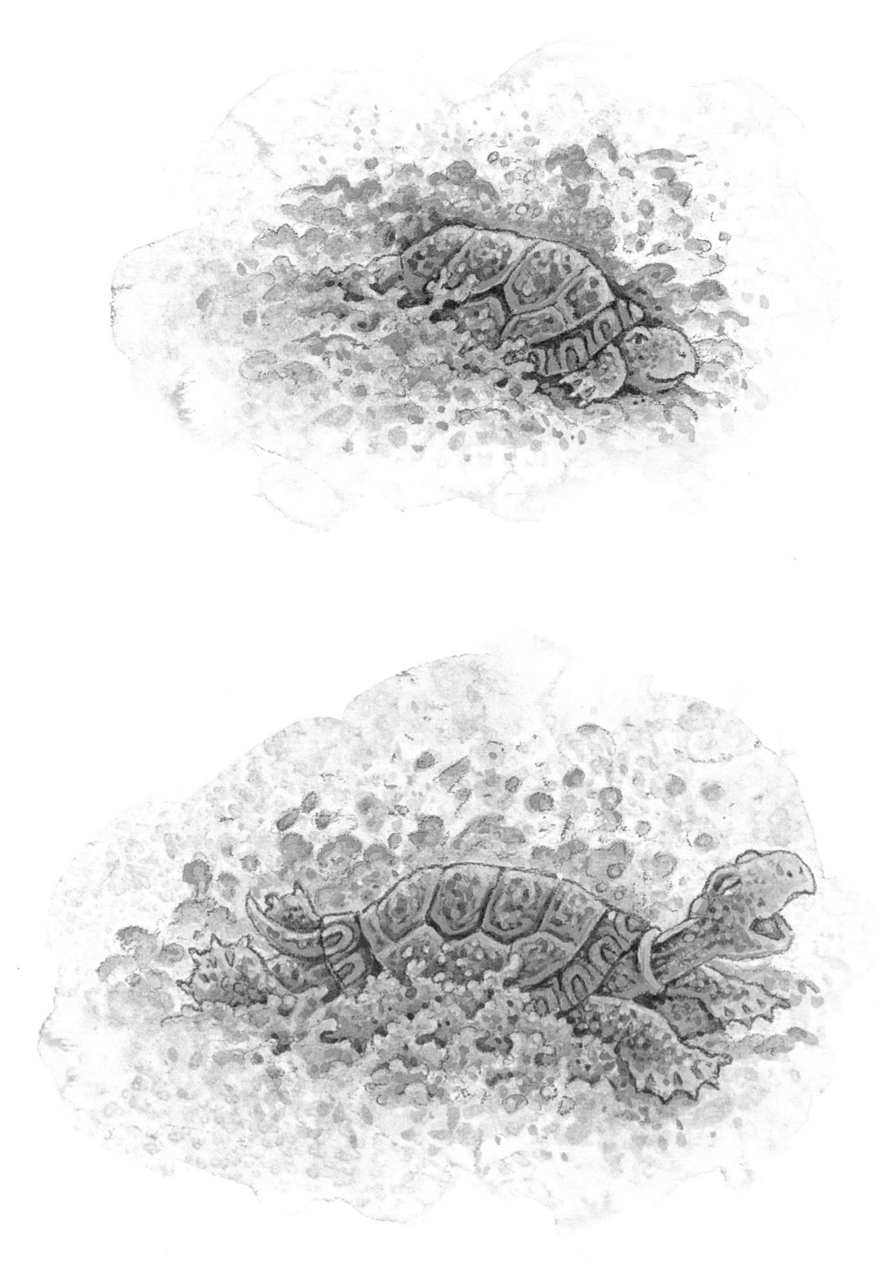

Where she dreamed of stretching.

Where she dreamed of climbing
out of the mud.

First she slid down an icy bank.

She turned a flip in the snow.

Then she dreamed
she climbed a tree.
She climbed to the farthest tip
of the highest branch of the tallest
tree in the entire forest.

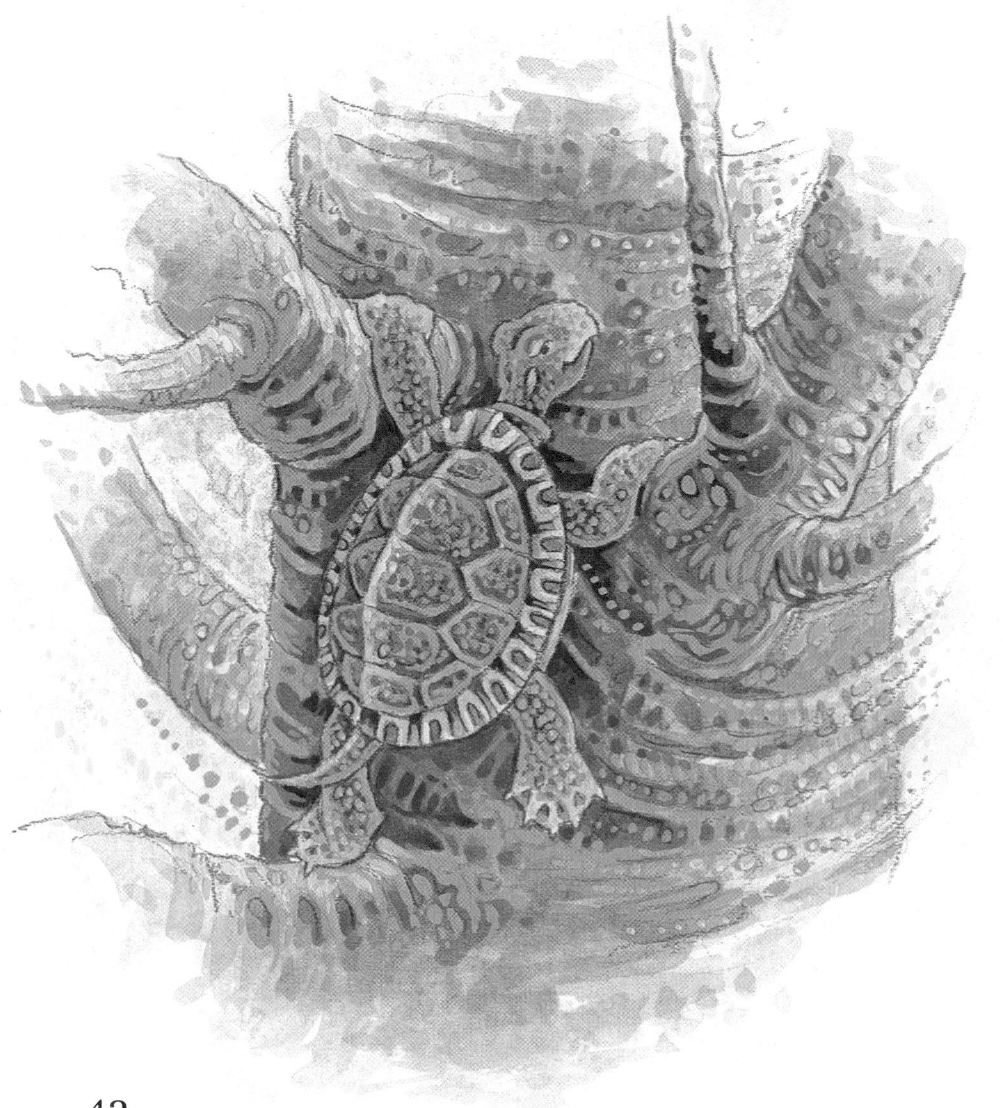

She sat there nibbling nuts.
The nuts tasted like sunshine,
all golden and warm.

When Turtle dropped,
the good air caught her.
It lifted her high.
So she turned another flip,
because a turtle can dream
anything.

Then she dreamed the best
dream of all.
It was a dream just made for a turtle.
She lay on a warm rock
at the edge of a cool pond.
She stretched her neck.
She twitched her tail.
She wiggled inside her shell.

And she smiled.

It was fine being a turtle in winter.